# Allan Ahlberg
# Treasure Hunt

*Illustrated by*

# Gillian Tyler

WALKER BOOKS
AND SUBSIDIARIES
LONDON • BOSTON • SYDNEY

 Tilly loves treasure hunting.

Each morning

Tilly's mum hides Tilly's breakfast banana

somewhere in the kitchen.

And Tilly hunts for it,

and hunts for it …

and *finds* it.

"My treasure!" cries Tilly.

And she eats it up.

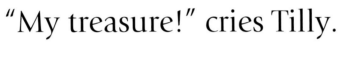

After breakfast

Tilly's dad hides

Tilly's rabbit somewhere in the garage.

And Tilly hunts for him,

and hunts for him …

and *finds* him.

"My treasure!" cries Tilly.

And she cuddles him up.

Sometimes when the snow falls …

Tilly's cat hides *herself*

in the garden.

And Tilly hunts for her,

"Here, Kitty!"

And hunts for her …

and *finds* her.

"Miaow!"

On Tilly's birthday

Tilly's grandma hides

five gold-wrapped coins of

chocolate money somewhere in the house.

And Tilly hunts for them,

and hunts for them,

and hunts for them,

and hunts for them,

and hunts for them …

and eats the lot.

Sometimes when the
weather is fine Tilly walks
with her mum and dad in the woods.

And *sometimes* her mum and dad

hide *themselves*.

But Tilly just hunts for them …

and finds them

straightaway.

"Easy peasy!" cries Tilly.

Before bedtime

Tilly's dad hides

Tilly's rabbit again,

this time in the garden.

And Tilly hunts for him,

and hunts for him …

and *finds* him.

"My treasure!"

cries Tilly.

And she carries

him upstairs.

Then ... bedtime.

Tilly's mum and dad sit reading the papers.

"Hm," says Tilly's dad.

"I wonder where Tilly has got to?"

"That's just what I was thinking,"

says Tilly's mum.

So Tilly's mum and dad hunt for Tilly.

And hunt for her,

"Wherever can she be?"

And hunt for her,

"I can't think where to look!"

And hunt for her, "Oh, dear!"

And hunt for her,

up and down

the house …

and *find* her.

"My treasure!"

cries Tilly's mum.

"My treasure too!"

cries Tilly's dad.

And they cuddle her up.

for Evie May McGown ~ G.T.

First published 2002 by Walker Books Ltd
87 Vauxhall Walk, London SE11 5HJ

1 2 3 4 5 6 7 8 9 10

Text © 2002 Allan Ahlberg
Illustrations © 2002 Gillian Tyler

This book has been typeset in Giovanni

Printed in Hong Kong

British Library Cataloguing in Publication Data:
a catalogue record for this book
is available from the British Library

ISBN 0-7445-7516-8